PURPLE

201 QUOTES ABOUT LOVE, LIFE, BEAUTY, WOMEN & HOPES

FIROZ TATA

DEDICATING TO THE ONE WHOM I WORSHIP AND WHOSE NAME I KEEP CHANTING.

LOVE YOU 'HEART' FOREVER. THANK YOU.

LOVE IS CRUEL, YET ASTOUNDINGLY ETERNAL!

Contents

Preface

Although the preface or the note from the author is the first part of the book that you read, it is the last that I wrote for my wonderful readers in India and overseas. Before going into any details, let me tell you that purple is my favourite colour as far as I remember since I was 8 or 10.

For most people, no date is more important than celebrating their birthdays or anniversaries. However, surely not for me. Four decades ago, although I was born on 16th July, I consider my real birth to be on 24th April. Strange or senseless it's up to you to decide. Years ago, for me, 24th April became a date to remember forever. Why? It happens to be the date I accidently crossed my path with Purple (with the grace of God) who fortunately or unfortunately (I am not sure) became the permanent occupant (24/7) of my heart. Readers, everyone has their unique life-story, so do I. However, someday, several heartwarming and heartbreaking stories I'll narrate to you all, perhaps a few decades later in my autobiography.

Creating quotes, poems and stories does involve some sort of worldly or writing experiences or a handsome understanding and strong command over a language. However, for me it also involves a roller coaster of strong emotions carefully blended in hours of solitude and engrossed pondering to select the perfect combinations of vocabulary while creating them.

Dear readers, it gives me endless ecstasy and satisfaction to present my fourth quote book 'Purple' in your hands. I am confident that even this book will serve its purpose in paving a long and successful path in recognizing, spreading and understanding the beautiful emotion of true and innocent love among generations to come. However, love is something that discovers the hidden beauty of a real human in you.

The book is created by keeping in mind the image of a very beautiful and extremely extraordinary 'Golden Hearted Unforgettable Purple' who resides in my mind, soul and heart. Once again, I would like to extend my genuine gratitude and life-long blessings to her for bestowing so much unexpected affection that I had hardly felt in life. She has always unknowingly helped me to visualize, conceive and birth the best of my creations in the form of numerous poems, stories and quotes.

For the sake of my contentment, I worship her, chant her name on those long sleepless nights, and yes, she is my strongest writing inspiration from a far distance. She is an absolute astounding beauty but not like those high heels super models. She is beautiful for the way she sees the dark world around her lone heart. She is beautiful for the way she ignites sparks in her brown bright eyes when she narrates something she passionately loves. She is beautiful for her extraordinary ability to make others heal, even if her unhealed heart is walled by doubts and darkness. No, she isn't beautiful for something as temporary as her sensual looks. She is beautiful inside out with her rare naked soul that belongs only to that fortunate person she fondly loves.

However, I have created nearly 800 quotes and many of them are already published on **yourquotes.in**. Just like my first three books of quotes, 'The Connecting Hearts', '16 June' (extremely popular among nationwide readers) and 'Forehead Forever', even this book is the result of several months of scribbling and evolving the exact grouping of vocabulary to build each quote. I have tried my level best not only to portray the feelings of love and beauty, but also the sentiments and values of hope, determination and patience through my various brainchild expressions.

I am confident that 'Purple' will generate hearty vibrations among my readers through the significant collection of my emotional and thought-provoking quotes. Those who find it difficult to articulate their emotions through words will feel encouraged to share my quotes with someone they deeply miss, care, admire, love, worship and are determined to have them in life one day.

The quotes in this book are purely creative thoughts based on my experiences, feelings and imagination. Any resemblance to other writings is completely unintentional and coincidental.

Hey, lads, lasses and lovers of all ages; don't forget to spread your million-dollar smile and positivity after reading my books. Kindly, without fail share your valuable reviews on **reviewmypublications@gmail.com.**

- The Author

(Mumbai, 24/4/2022)

not only to portray the feelings of love and beauty, but also the sentiments and values of hope, determination and patience through my various brainchild expressions.

I am confident that Purple will generate hearty vibrations among my readers through the significant collection of my emotional and thought-provoking quotes. Those who find it difficult to articulate their emotions through words will feel encouraged to share my quotes with someone they deeply miss, care, admire, love, worship and are determined to have them in life one day.

The quotes in this book are purely creative thoughts based on [illegible] and [illegible]. Any [illegible] coincidental.

Hey, lads, lasses and lovers of all ages, don't forget to spread your million-dollar smile and positivity after reading my books. Kindly, without fail share your [illegible] reviews on [illegible]

Acknowledgements

No one may write such acknowledgements, but I do for my readers...

From deep down my core, I express gratitude to my old and exhausted soul for someway continuing to love writing by undergoing almost day-to-day household turbulences, pointless responsibilities, forcefully sparing ample time for others to do their various tasks and heartlessly welcoming stress from loved ones that can end life any day through mental or physical collapse. However, for their good, I am still alive.

Without fail, I would love to extend my deepest appreciation and acknowledgement to a beautiful found and lost Purple whom my readers will surely discover and feel again through most of my quotes. Every quote is delicately created by me in this heart-warming book.

- The Author

♡♡♡

1

Quotes Cluster - A

Writing a quote isn't only a feeling that is expressed, as it can be a craving cry of a massacred heart that mouth miserably fails to utter.

Waiting, and just waiting forever is the silent strength in strangled hands when one refuses to stop loving.

Loving another was never an option when missing the one was so damaging each night.

Any craving man can treat a woman right for a night, but it takes a gentleman to treat her aptly for the rest of his life.

Admire a man who is ready to heal a heart that he never broke and raise a child that his semen didn't create.

Rods of acidic rain fell around her as a curtain of shivering glass enchanting the scars on her soul making her astoundingly beautiful.

♡♡♡

Just as he had no money and fame like her, she had no heart like him to hold his, gradually fading him in the invisible mist of sadness.

♡♡♡

It is very strange that those you have never met get so close to your heart compared to those who are ascribed as ours, having no time and interest in our life.

♡♡♡

Honestly speaking I deny having somebody who sees only the good in me as I have a distant one who loves every bad and imperfection in me.

♡♡♡

It's not with whom your life progresses towards the end. It's with whom your dumb heart finally decides to rest in peace, after life. Love eternally.

♡♡♡

2

Quotes Cluster - B

Short lustrous wavy hair tangling me by my thoughts.
She is my green earth after several spring rain drops.
Smouldering brown eyes, reading my heart like a map.
My gaze rested the day eyes beheld her stunning snap.

Self-made man can be dangerously determined and hard working, as he has mastered his skills of how to rise from his falls, flaws and failures.

His purpose in her life was to help her become a woman of dreams for another man.

So you see. Once a wise man said...
Sometimes the optimum way to make mouths shut is through your writings and not by speaking.
And that wise man was of course not me.

We hang over to their priority list based on our rank, as none of us can always stay busy.

♡♡♡

She was swept away by his charm and made him drown in her exquisite beauty; both intensely falling for each other and then falling apart eternally.

♡♡♡

It's more peaceful to stay unmarried than to wrongly marry and keep grumbling for the rest of life.

♡♡♡

Time turns our struggles into strength and scars into an astounding art.

♡♡♡

Any relation can be saved if we understand a simple fact that people are not wrong, they are just different from what we hope to expect.

♡♡♡

Man's optimal idea of love is to first respect a woman through his eyes and then his language.

♡♡♡

3

Quotes Cluster - C

The virtue of colossal patience makes a man appear sexier as without it he is a burning lamp with almost no oil. Patience attracts.

♡♡♡

Her whole-hearted honesty was something that appealed to me the most.

♡♡♡

One must try to love pains to get stronger as God's greatest blessing can sometimes arrive through utmost pain.

♡♡♡

Tell a few lies, soon all your truths will turn questionable.

♡♡♡

First to apologize, as she was the bravest. First to forgive, as she was the strongest.

♡♡♡

To stand in the hall of fame be that hardworking victor who never waits for a fortune turn.

ᑭᑭᑭ

Instead of grumbling all day long, count your blessings and be grateful to God for what he has already bestowed.

ᑭᑭᑭ

You can be easily fooled by one's modesty.

ᑭᑭᑭ

She is more than beautiful and never will be less than pretty, if you know what I mean.
A face to remember daily; preserved in my words and residing in my fondest memories.

ᑭᑭᑭ

There can never be anything more sweetly sexier in my woman than me holding her tender heart, witnessing her sheer simplicity and heartfelt humility; hysterically attracting me the most.

ᑭᑭᑭ

4

Quotes Cluster -D

Love should reside in one's mind, heart and soul and not necessarily in one's life.

The real exquisiteness of an unforgettable woman is seen in the sheen of her solitary somber eyes, as they are the doorways to her gale-forced windy heart, a place where her deep discovered love resides.

They miserably failed with a full stop, as they knew that semicolons and commas were the only best options to make their tangled tale more and more agonizingly interesting with the passage of years and then perhaps a few decades.

Loving her was euphoric at one moment and deep despair the other. I had never experienced such a turmoil.

Attachment is effortless.
Detachment demands power.

ᑭᑭᑭ

When you keep trying to satisfy everyone, you surely end up completely unsatisfied.

ᑭᑭᑭ

She may not always be appreciated and understood, but her insightfulness, empathetic power, deep contemplation and wittiness can never be challenged.

ᑭᑭᑭ

An unforgettable woman offers more than she receives and expects nothing in return besides admiration, love, care, respect, dignity and gratitude.

ᑭᑭᑭ

I earnestly believe that her splendour and beauty multiplies with the passage of time and years.

ᑭᑭᑭ

Physical and sexual links have almost zero gravity amid the soulmates as it heebie-jeebies their cores with the thought of parting and they do not ever want to say goodbye after crossing each other's paths.

ᑭᑭᑭ

5 Quotes Cluster - E

Dear fellow men,
Never underestimate the hidden might of a woman. She can be an unknown dormant volcano awaiting an abrupt eruption, swiping us burnt out of life.

At times, it's too tough to keep showing it's too easy.

If you ever loved me, you would have never raised hands on me, and if you raised your hands on me, unfortunately our love was actually never born.

Although her heart-hitting honesty was sometimes hurtful to read, it gracefully massacred his heart towards her love.

Can we be more respectful, irrespective of its reciprocal?

My dear destiny,
Let me dare to fall in love and birth from the ashes or bury my heart into the oceans of agony.

ꝒꝒꝒ

Sometimes you have to agree that your biggest supporters are someone whom you don't know personally and the biggest demoralizers (users) are those whom you know very well.

ꝒꝒꝒ

Deceptive beauty can be seen through her face, skin, attire, shoes and mild makeup she wears, but her never perishing beauty is only discovered through her big brown butterfly eyes, courteous tongue, deep yet innocent thoughts and her scarred heart that pounds just for the 'One'.
Lord's gifted grace to the blessed me.

ꝒꝒꝒ

One doesn't need her existence in life to sculpt words, as her intense impression on mind and panoramic portrait in heart is sufficient.

ꝒꝒꝒ

The hidden might of a discreet woman should never be dared, as she exactly knows what and whom she really needs in life.
She can be a deadly tigress pouncing on her long awaited prey.

ꝒꝒꝒ

Sometimes some waits are worth the wait, perhaps for just a simple 'Hello' from them.

Waiting is ecstatically eternal, as love has no alternative.

Then rare good memories once again energized in front of him like a crusade of brutal troops of enemies.

Love is nothing, loved is something and love and to be loved is everything.

The more you madly and deeply love the more they drastically disappear.
The more you run from them, the more they drown you into their awe-inspiring and breathtaking memories.

You may have felt neglected, lonely, torn apart, dejected, unappreciated and misjudged for the majority of your life, but meeting a soulmate erases all those aching agonies at a blink of an eye. After all, it's a cosmic connection.

♡♡♡

What made her grace look more graceful was neither her astonishing beauty nor ingenious appearance or what she had accomplished.

It was her oceanic love and audacity to believe that no matter the stormy long night around her soul, that brightest love-ray ran wild within her core.

It was the only way her soul once again came alive, showing in everything until today.

♡♡♡

Her mesmerizing beauty within was limitless just like her incredible innocence.

Her salty scars were more sexy than her divine body and her enchanting eyes spoke more than her luscious lips.

Her hurricane heart pounded more for him than her sacrificed soul could ever resist.

♡♡♡

Woman's naked heart, naked soul, naked smile, naked thoughts, naked opinions, naked eyes, naked words and naked believes are much erotic than her naked body.

♡♡♡

Survival with a picture in hand was easier than a permanent portrait engraved on a burnt heart.

♡♡♡

7

Quotes Cluster - G

Holding firmly for years wasn't awful, but embracing the anguish until was certainly.

♡♡♡

Underestimate a deadly determined man who is perhaps on the verge to lose. I swear, it'll be a massive fun.

♡♡♡

A person who repeatedly denies departing your mind is the hostage that has arrived to reside forever in your heart.

♡♡♡

Probably it wasn't the hardest part to break the news to an already broken heart.

♡♡♡

The more you tell lies, the more you have to remember. The more you try to remember, the more you fumble and multiply lies further.

♡♡♡

It's abruptly staggering to comprehend. It's just an ending. This isn't our dead end.

ᑭᑭᑭ

Never light a ray of love-hope in someone until you aren't brave enough to burn in with them while providing lifelong warmth to both.

ᑭᑭᑭ

If you wish to be captivatingly heard, first learn to listen.

ᑭᑭᑭ

Suppressed persistence is more dangerous, deadly than a tracer bullet travelling to tear apart its target.

ᑭᑭᑭ

In fact, the more they think they know about me, the less they know anything about me.

ᑭᑭᑭ

8

Quotes Cluster - H

Memories that are unwilling to move forward are impossible to erase from one's mind.

ღღღ

Living a simple and minimal life means...
You have less to lose, less to be disturbed by and less dependency on other things in your life.

ღღღ

While training my mind to be strong over my feelings, finally I lost myself to me.

ღღღ

A failure that turns you humble is better than a triumph that makes you arrogant.

ღღღ

The multiplication of misery added strength to steer until the year they finally met forever.

ღღღ

Don’t think if you can speak a particular language somewhat fluently, you are gifted to express your deepest thoughts through writings.

Writing requires observational skills, at least one beautiful heartbreak, tortuous pondering practice; and not merely the speaking skills.

My creations could never be created if God had not created that ‘Heart’ to cross through my story for a thousand years and yet another thousand to come.

You’ll vanquish when you decide to thrive under the thunder conceiving possible out of just impossible.

Portraitist permanently portrayed his name on her vena amoris, the vein of love, keeping them invisibly connected.

I am not what you know, but what you’ll soon see, and surely my dear, you don’t need to care, until I let you.

9

Quotes Cluster - I

At some point, I believe it's worthy to stay uneducated, rather than having shortsighted, corrupt, demanding, mean, selfish, damaging and tormenting teachers. I encountered several.

Their destinies were left with no other option but to face the dilemma of bending its ruthless rules, making them finally meet always and forever.

A determined person is someone that keeps walking no matter how long and hard the path might seem. He knows that the next turn can take him to his destination.

Five years and a volcanic calm ocean between us with unfinished whirlpool words at two distant horizons, but with a strong denial of never losing hopes of togetherness.

To be conclusive and strong, you must be willing to take accountability for your actions. You must be willing to survive with the consequences of your choices.

ᑭᑭᑭ

Love is a stubborn decision and not a foolish emotion.

ᑭᑭᑭ

When a man truly loves, he acts like a child looking for a different kind of nurture.
When a woman truly loves, she acts like a mother guiding him at every difficult step.

ᑭᑭᑭ

Silence loudly talks without words, but in our mind.

ᑭᑭᑭ

Fake a shipwreck to get rid of rats from life.
Isn't that genius!

ᑭᑭᑭ

Neither night could stop painting her purple portrait that was desperately incomplete, nor did the mind give up its attempt to canvas it, until finally they did one day.

ᑭᑭᑭ

10

Quotes Cluster - J

Too many material possessions will ultimately sacrifice your freedom resulting into overly accustomed to comforts that won't always last.

The smarter is the one who actually doesn't think he/she is.

Weak people end with multiple lovers.
Strong ones with one.

Dear men,
It is easier to attract a loyal woman through hard work and brains than deceptive looks and polished pockets.

You'll rescue the one you really love, even at the cost of your own life.

Soulful lines touched their souls; thousands could touch the writer's. Sensual scars forced to fall for, none, but only the one faraway fighter.

To pen down you don't need a supreme educational tail of degrees behind your name, rich clothes, sophisticated living or esteemed designated status in the society.

I have none of these things besides basic education blended in the hearty feelings wrapped in the rainbow of her soul setting a long tail of my writing goals.

A true lover is not someone that depends on magic or miracles to make things happen, but someone that believes in magic and in miracles, and convinces a strong faith towards making those happen.

A woman's pleasing face attracts a flirty, her curvy body attracts a jerk, her unhealed heart attracts a lover and her charismatic character attracts a man to love her.

The modern and the best way to spill lies around:
'Oh! I absolutely forgot!'

11

Quotes Cluster -K

Powerful life lessons are learned with less money that at times prosperous people miserably fail to understand.

♡♡♡

It would be better for me to be a vile villain in someone's story, than be a dejected hero handcuffed, waiting for the first opportunity.

♡♡♡

The best way to fool them is by staying at your lowest key.

♡♡♡

'Missing you' isn't enough to express the unseen yet strongly felt silent suffering that gulps one daily.

♡♡♡

And then yet another night falls testing the endurance and scorching adrenal strength that one should not dare to take it for granted.

♡♡♡

The recovery was out of question once it was touched by her graceful heart.

ᕈᕈᕈ

It is better to love the heart that reciprocates the same in return than to forcefully glue around the old stick in the mud relation.

ᕈᕈᕈ

It is one of the sweetest and sacred things to be unconditionally loved.

ᕈᕈᕈ

A lover is not someone who rushes to vanquish love, but someone that has a strong willpower and always ready to sacrifice for the other.

ᕈᕈᕈ

Dear Love,
Time won't always remain the same, your outside beauty will flee one day.
Time will arrive; your thick black hair will gradually turn thin and grey.
Tight and fair skin will wrinkle day-by-day.
Surely, I'll keep kissing your fabulous forehead, madly love and indeed always care the same way.
I may not always be so humble and kind. Someday, I might be grumpy and bitter, but will always be your ruddy lips sweet wine.

ᕈᕈᕈ

12

Quotes Cluster - L

Although then I may never be around you, but I promise my writings will so very much shield you each night until I finally meet you in paradise.

ᦗᦗᦗ

Loving so right at such a wrong time is an unforgiving battle that he faced until his final sunset at life's horizon.

ᦗᦗᦗ

It was so solitary and creepy as without her my surroundings felt so weepy and sleepy.
Her silhouette left invading me with blackness, forcing me to bow my head in her love's blindness.

ᦗᦗᦗ

It's somewhat bearable to let your love weightily be with another, than to dejectedly surrender the hurricane hopes of never being together. Love has bizarre bending rules that can be desecrated anytime.

ᦗᦗᦗ

Unconditional love is a fervent devotion, cultivating a powerful virtue in any individual.

♡♡♡

Invest time and energy only in those who are willing and show signs to return the same.

♡♡♡

It may take years for our hopes to be fulfilled, but will just take a while to be content abruptly one day.

♡♡♡

I believe, when you surely know it's the only best for you... get ready to cross the line without any hesitation.

♡♡♡

She is a guaranteed grace, making their hurricane hearts race. Astoundingly amazing, making a dead devil alive from ashes. A miraculous melody, making dumb man's heart dance. And ridiculously beautiful, making beauty itself shameful. She is my loving lady.

♡♡♡

Do not try to impress or influence with your lies as it doesn't last long for the one who is in love to observe and rethink over every situation.

♡♡♡

13

Quotes Cluster - M

He who flatters and flirts, rolls his eyes after her body. He, who listens deep and loves loyally, holds her heart and soul, eternally.

♡♡♡

Merely being married is not a matter of wishing to be married as it is a matter of mastering the art of leading a long-lasting blissful relationship.

♡♡♡

Although, for now, my weapons to succeed are blunt. Be sadly mistaken, I do have what it takes to uplift myself again.

♡♡♡

Mastering, moulding and merging the words for a beautiful formation is as challenging as making someone else's unhappy wife officially yours; forever. However, both attainable with patience, perseverance, passion and purity.

♡♡♡

A person eager to succeed is an unstoppable and determined sweet devil in disguise.

♡♡♡

Sipping some sweet tea with sad songs whirling into her whirlpool mind, adding further grace to his perfectly crafted natural-divine.

Her amazing beauty, my eyes rode through the halls of heaven, feeling ecstatic.

Her missing presence generating deep agony within that I could hardly resist.

♡♡♡

It's divine to be forever loved by an unexpected one, making it more divine to reciprocate the same with passion, escalating into two-way loyal love.

♡♡♡

Once a man's heart is soulfully touched by a woman, it's never possible for yet another touch by the other, and as a persistent man, I assure you.

♡♡♡

Love prevails by bowing down the rules set by the power of money and influence.

♡♡♡

It is not important that yesterday I was badly defeated, but it is surely dangerous that I decided to kiss the dusty ground and get up once again to rewrite my own story.

♡♡♡

14
Quotes Cluster -VI

Loving someone is not about money and material things, but about tenderly nurturing the heart and soul that you can never afford to lose.

Not trying at all is the most devastating failure a person can usually encounter.

Chipper voice, blossoming fresh morning feelings for me.
'Good morning' still whispers from a woman I want to glue.
Captivating, I firmly believed; only she's my peppy jig,
searched since warm winds whistled through the tree-twigs.

If you frantically need something you never had, you must be willing to do something very courageously you have never done all life.

The more failures I encounter, the stronger they'll sculpt me to thrive towards my final destination to have you in my empty arms. Never challenge a determined person.

You said, 'Please move on'. The stubborn I said, 'Will never'. My love, we are the two hanging hearts that are now tangled together, always and forever.

A true lover keeps battling in the face of fear.

Surrounded by dependent innocent idiots is like a dangling walk on a rope, blindfolded.

A few days apart, needed her more than ever.
He felt her angelic whiff in the garden-fresh air like a loyal lover.
Imagining her presence more than previous occasions.
Cherished her existence more than anyone.

The worst life-threatening blunder is to undervalue the unseen and take everything too lightly.

15

Quotes Cluster - O

Craven falls for illicit affairs.
Valiant falls in devoted love that lasts forever, but through the hurtful paths towards end.

It's all right to have a million storms in your hurricane heart than in your life.

A man can never be loved as equal as his mother and by anyone more than that very special woman who is madly in love with him. It's precious.

For me, the outer simplicity of a woman is the highest form of her simplest sophistication.

A new beginning always awaits at the other side of the end.

My woman is a delicate dictionary with deep, dark, delightful secrets concealed under her dazzling smile. Although hard to learn, yet easy to read if I keep turning her pages patiently and respectfully.

ღღღ

Colourful butterflies fluttered around her sparkling and blissful elegance. She reclined on her easy chair, gazing at her mangoes and coconuts.

Birds chirping around, soon a few moments of silence, giving solace and serenity to her mental violence.

ღღღ

My emptiness:

Surrounded by many noisy vessels, but failing and refusing to make noise like them, giving birth to a beautiful uniqueness.

ღღღ

Love is a remarkable occurrence and hope to succeed in it is an astounding phenomena.

ღღღ

Dare not dangle danger over your head by keeping her at stake. I am an animal of her choice, her loving wolf.

ღღღ

16

Quotes Cluster - D

A woman who finally discovers her real worth in society becomes unstoppable.

Sometimes it's too late to think and sometimes it's never too late to rethink to start again, resulting into a gradual yet massive transformation.

It's beautiful to love and perhaps never be together than to live together and never love.

A man must feel pride and ecstasy in keeping his woman ahead of himself, fulfilling her wishes first than his.

Turning a fortune through dedication and hard work is not like turning a page of a book, with a blink of an eye.

It's a worst mistake to leave your enemy half defeated and half dead.

ÞÞÞ

Distance whispered me that,
'The real meaning of proximity is not the existing presence alongside, but a hope that our heart illuminates that it'll be surely someday.'

ÞÞÞ

A complex love relation sometimes requires pondering in some simple terms.

ÞÞÞ

A warm warning through words is better than a vile action of destruction.

ÞÞÞ

Certain love connections that are above time and space are spellbindingly supernatural.

ÞÞÞ

17

Quotes Cluster - 2

Her feelings were wrapped under the moonlit night sky, encircled by the massive mountains on all four sides.
She had turned into a deep-rooted snow-clad tree enduring the frigid winds, now turning into my purple lagoon-lotus, vision could barely reach.

♡♡♡

He is a man, man enough not to love a million girls as he loves to love only one in a million ways.
And surely, that's for only you, my 'Heart'!

♡♡♡

Be your own solitary lover, least expecting to be heartily loved by any one.

♡♡♡

It's better to be a broken and busted heart lonely lover than a posh pocket hideous hearted husband who never appreciates or acknowledges his wife.

♡♡♡

True beauty in a woman is echoed through her tranquil yet thunderous soul.

Sometimes what just kills you within teaches you to be stronger to survive.

She was just like a partly dead unhappy flower somehow surviving in her deserted world filled with several riches.

Although you may be drowning daily, to keep loved ones ever protected you have to opt for a self-sacrifice.
That is called 'Love'.

Lying flawlessly is a crafty art as it's not everybody's cup of coffee.

Have been there with me from the time I learned to hold you. You beheld my desires and dreams the delighted devil tried to chew. If you had emotions, you would have embraced my frail parts.

My precious pen, for now I have no one to mend my broken heart.

18

Quotes Cluster - R

In today's world, any person can be a nightmare disguised-dressed in a daydream.

It's awful and agonizingly sad when you no longer can be your own self to the one you have forever known. Will you ever understand this?

The firm will of God is often what we call fate.

Only perseverance pressures progress towards our goals and accomplishments.

To the entire world, you may be one person or a person with a few faces, but to the one you truly love you may always be the one you actually are.

When we do not face criticism, we begin to grow overconfident, which is not uplifting in nature.

ღღღ

A sleepless human mind is a place for devil's delight.

ღღღ

Sometimes we are just a decision away from a very different kind of life.

ღღღ

The one who learns to adjust the surroundings knows the process of survival.

ღღღ

Ride away with me; stroll the midtown silent street, and tell me that we do not feel dizzy.
Forehead fascinating gracious scintillating is she, riding at night, seeing the world so specific.
You never know if you never ride so, ride away with me and say ciao to a ride so sassy.

ღღღ

19

Quotes Cluster - S

She possessing inner beauty is an ever joy for him.

I am not defeated unless I believe and accept I am and an honest man's words are as good as his indestructible bond with his love.

Desperately trying not to love you only makes me fondly love you more.

He was never a coward, but cautious to distant deliberate. A farsighted fighter to walk her down the aisle the day destinies were compelled to kneel down, accepting their long awaited love.

The first person to check the level of your quality is you.

Her dejected eyes deceived her the most as they couldn't stop screening what her ancient soul had buried within her heart for years.

ᑭᑭᑭ

Offering a genuine psychological and emotional support is the primary key to cultivate a long-lasting fruitful relation.

ᑭᑭᑭ

A true soulmate hangs onto our every word and thus we feel noticeable, appreciated and cherished, making us feel comfortable by graciously holding our heart and soul.

ᑭᑭᑭ

Over the years, the pain was real, finally forgiving them to start the gradual process of self-healing.

How close the end was, well no one knew, as the future is a mystery enveloped in disguise.

ᑭᑭᑭ

You just don't need to be physically together with the person you feel romantic as adding them into your daily prayers is the purest form to prove that they are invisibly present with you romancing deep down into the core of your heart.

A prayer is the potent property of your love.

ᑭᑭᑭ

20

Quotes Cluster -T

God's creations are always matchless and magnificent.

Evolving a fighter mindset is complex and comprises a number of different strategies and actions.

Ecstasy is a feeling or state of great joy that transforms life's bleakness into brightness.
It has countless powerful forms that depend on us to bring it out even through various life storms.

The yield of hopes will certainly harvest, rejoicing for several seasons.
Penning down the gloomiest cloud thundering over mind, thanking God for His divine existence.
Filling the vacuum; seeing the falling night, stars glittering in the mighty sky, finally sleeping with its sight.

Marry when your soul finally falls for, neither your heart nor the demanding age.

♡♡♡

True love in a bizarre way is the water that finds its way by swiftly drifting over and around several obstacles.

♡♡♡

Uniqueness also includes meeting appreciation, creating one's own tale and spreading inspiration.
Recognize the enchanted magic you possess and only you have the authority for its access.

♡♡♡

Never mistake her compassion as her weakness.

♡♡♡

A 'Tata' is a Tata through a brainy brain breathing within his unhealed heart and not by his ascribed second name 'Tata'.

♡♡♡

Byes and goodbyes prove to be merely two meaningless words when two souls are already intertwined in everlasting love.

♡♡♡

My million words will surely reach its final destination and perhaps the world will recall appreciating after I am gone. That's how my dumb love will finally begin its long awaited work, after life.

♡♡♡

21

An Unforgettable Purple Heart

My Dear Readers,

Once Eleanor Roosevelt, an American political figure said, "A woman is like a tea bag. You never know how strong she is until she gets in hot water." however, for me, the beauty of an unforgettable woman is not in the clothes she wears, makeup she puts on, her overall looks, figure she carries or the way she maintains her hair. The real exquisiteness of an unforgettable woman is seen in the sheen of her solitary somber eyes, as they are the doorways to her gale-forced windy heart, a place where her deep discovered love resides. True beauty in a woman is echoed through her tranquil yet thunderous soul. It is the caring nature that she holds within, affectionately validates her passion that she keeps showing under any circumstances life tosses.

It is earnestly believed that her splendour and beauty grows with the passage of years. One can find eye-candy beautiful women everywhere, but coming across a soul-candy unforgettable woman is once in a lifetime rare fortune, not less than a miracle. Well, one cannot speak for every woman; but the probabilities are that she is tired of dating and befriending one and dealing with one after another run-of-the-mill person. She is tired of being taken for granted, advantaged, lied, mistreated, misunderstood, unappreciated, unacknowledged, disrespected, uncared, offended and doubted. Her soul injuries and sacrifices are deeper than the scars her body withstands most part of her life. An unforgettable woman has several buried, suppressed, undiscovered, restricted and spectacularly awesome potentials. These qualities are usually the kind-hearted and blindfold trusting types that are unfortunately too often exploited by society. Gradually she turns into a dry flower in a deserted world.

A cherished woman is the one whose family, friends or partner, curse themselves for letting her go or losing her from their lives. However, her hidden extraordinary potentials are not that easy to read by an ordinary man. It is an unfortunate fact evident throughout her life.

Her kindness is obvious in whatever she does and wherever she goes. No matter how many times her thought, generosity and pleasantness have gone overlooked, she refuses to quit and continues. She touches peoples' lives and hearts more than words can ever express. If she is fortunate enough to find a good life partner, chances are she falls in a lifetime of unconditional love. However, she is a strong woman who refuses to value her worth from her partner. The exclusive potentials that she holds are true to her heart.

An unforgettable woman offers more than she receives and expects nothing in return besides admiration, love, care, respect, dignity and gratitude. Think of a significant woman in your life; a woman who loves you more than anyone. Ask yourself a simple question. Has she never kept her own needs aside before yours? She always carries herself with divine grace and elegance. Your mother is the finest example in the first place.

Whether she is a family member, a friend or a partner, her support is never artificial and it never appears to cease. Though she may not always agree with the things going around her, still she will show her support. She may not always be appreciated and understood, but her insightfulness, empathetic power, deep contemplation and wittiness can never be challenged.

An unforgettable woman loves to face the world head-on with keenness. While she may not be very loud, her optimistic attitude and brilliance should always be sincerely appreciated and cared for. She may be very sugary, but she is never afraid to show some of her sour taste when needed. Sometimes, this flavour comes after someone mistakes her compassion for weakness. For the most part of her life, her honest words are delivered in equal parts, sweet and solemn.

About The Author

FIROZ TATA is a non-practicing priest, an author, a poet, notion creator, a storyteller and a national level cyclist from Mumbai, India. He is credited to win several prestigious medals and trophies in the sport of cycling. He has been fascinating his nationwide readers with his academic as well as fictional writings for nearly 15 years.

He has shown his strong writing influence through informative and imaginative essays, instructive letters, heart-warming poems, engrossing stories as well as captivating quotes depicting resolve, love, women, beauty and hopes. However, he is a single man, perhaps patiently waiting for someone. He firmly believes to love and to be loved loyally and passionately from a distance rather than sticking in an intolerable and suffocative relationship.

Due to his deserted, suppressive and cut off childhood and adolescent years from the outer world, he had no other alternative but to develop a deep passion and skills for writing since his early days. Back then, as a child, he was destined to encounter numerous terrible experiences with his several teachers. He also had his share of horrible experiences at home that no child deserves.

After failing miserably in English in the last and decisive year of his schooling, no one but only him through the burning desire, dedication and determination in his heart knew that one day he would become a published author. Years later, he successfully did. Even today, he is dedicated on the path of enriching himself with knowledge and improving with the passing years.

By now, he has authored nearly 60 academic as well as fictional books for various nationwide publishers. His works also include nearly 500 essays and 800 quotes in his total 15 creative writing books. His books are strongly recommended not only for the bookshelves of children, but also adults. His works are highly appreciated and acclaimed by several readers, educationalists and publishers.

Printed by Libri Plureos GmbH in Hamburg,
Germany